Josiah Gilbert Holland

The Puritan Guest

And other Poems

Josiah Gilbert Holland

The Puritan Guest
And other Poems

ISBN/EAN: 9783741187377

Manufactured in Europe, USA, Canada, Australia, Japa

Cover: Foto ©Andreas Hilbeck / pixelio.de

Manufactured and distributed by brebook publishing software
(www.brebook.com)

Josiah Gilbert Holland

The Puritan Guest

THE PURITAN'S GUEST

AND OTHER POEMS

J. G. HOLLAND

NEW YORK
CHARLES SCRIBNER'S SONS
1885

TROW'S
PRINTING AND BOOKBINDING COMPANY,
NEW YORK.

CONTENTS.

iv   CONTENTS.

THE PURITAN'S GUEST.

I.

THE house stood back from the old Bay
    Road
That wound through Sudbury town ;
Before it a brawling streamlet flowed ;
    Behind it the woods shut down.

Dwelt there the Puritan, good John Guye,
    With the daughters God had given,—
Three beautiful maidens fair and shy,
    Whose mother was in heaven.

1

And one was Patience, so tall and fair ;
   And one was queenly Prue ;
And one was Hope with the golden hair ;
   And the eyes of all were blue.

And horsemen, riding along that way,
   Drank at the household spring,
And asked of the maids the time o' day,
   Or brought them news of the King.

It seemed like a glimpse of heaven to see,
   In sun and storm the same,
These three fair maidens at windows three
   To the riders who went and came.

It seemed like an hour in heaven to sit,
   When the winter wind blew hoarse,
And watch these diligent maidens knit,
   And hear John Guye's discourse.

If love was lighted, ah, who may say !—
  It was centuries ago ;—
And maids were the same in the olden day
  That they are now, I trow.

And who shall wonder, or who condemn—
  For their life had scanty zest—
If dangerous fancies came to them,
  As the men rode east and west ?

Guye ruled his house by the olden law,
  And he knew the heart of a maid ;
And, watching with godly care, he saw
  What made his soul afraid !

For smiles shone up from the saucy lips
  That drank at the household spring,
And kisses were tossed from finger-tips
  With the tidings of the King.

And the eyes that should have flamed with
    fire,
  And spurned these gallant arts,
Grew soft and sad with a strange desire,
  Over tender and troubled hearts.

" Ah God ! " groaned the Puritan, good John
    Guye,
  " That such a woe can be !—
That their mother should be in heaven, and I
  Should be left with daughters three ! "

(And one was Patience, so tall and fair ;
  And one was queenly Prue ;
And one was Hope with the golden hair ;
  And the eyes of all were blue.)

II.

From the bitter sea it had blown all day,
  And the night came hurrying down ;
And snow from a sky all cold and gray
  Was whitening Sudbury town.

The chimney roared like an angry beast,
  With eyes and tongues of fire,
And the crazy windows facing east
  Shook in the tempest's ire.

The sleety snow fell heavy and fast ;
  It beat on the roof like rain ;
And the forest hurtled beneath the blast
  Of the dreadful hurricane !

The autumn leaves that had flown all day,
  In wild and scurrying flocks,
Were pelted down by the hail, and lay
  Huddled among the rocks.

" 'Tis a fearful storm!" said good John
    Guye,
  As he looked at his daughters three ;
" And the riders abroad to-night must die ;
  And many such there be ! "

Their cheeks grew pale in the ruddy blaze
  With what their ears had heard,
And they looked in the fire with grieved
    amaze ;
  But they could not speak a word.

(And one was Patience, so tall and fair ;
  And one was queenly Prue ;
And one was Hope with the golden hair ;
  And the eyes of all were blue.)

'Twas an owl flew hooting out of the trees,
  In a lull of the tempest's wrath ;
And caught mid-air by the crafty breeze,
  He wrestled for his path.

He wrestled long, but he strove in vain
  With the fierce and blinding gloom ;
He was shot like a bolt through the window-
    pane,
  And a great gust filled the room.

They sprang to their feet in sharp affright,
  But still no word they said,
As they stopped the window from the night;
  And the great white bird lay dead!

" 'Tis a fearful storm!" said good John
      Guye ;
  " Heaven help all those abroad !
For the men who ride, and the birds that fly,
  Let us kneel and pray to God ! "

But while they knelt, and the hoary saint
  Groaned with the stress of prayer,
They heard from a wanderer, far and faint,
  A shriek of wild despair.

"Thank God!" said the Puritan, rising
      straight ;
  " Thank God, my daughters three,
That the answer of heaven does not wait,
  And my guest has come to me ! "

He flung to the wall the oaken door ;
  He passed it with a bound ;
And plunging into the darkness frore,
  He listened along the ground.

Prone on the path he found his guest ;
  His hair was streaming wild ;
Guye lifted him to his mighty breast
  As he had been a child.

The maidens three peered into the storm ;
  It smote their brows like death ;
They saw their father's stalwart form ;
  They heard his struggling breath.

(And one was Patience, so tall and fair ;
  And one was queenly Prue ;
And one was Hope with the golden hair ;
  And the eyes of all were blue.)

They laid the stranger before the flame,
  They nursed him till he stirred,—
Till he opened his eyes, and spoke a name!—
  'Twas a woman's name they heard !

They nursed him long with tender care,
  The while he moaned and wept ;
He wakened anon to breathe a prayer
  And anon he sank and slept.

The ghostly shade of a man he seemed ;
  His teeth were white as milk ;
And the long white curls on his forehead
    gleamed
  Like skeins of tangled silk.

His eyes peered out with an eerie stare,—
  They were wondrous deep and large,—
And they looked like mountain tarns aglare
  Beneath their beetling marge !

He rose straight up from his lowly bed ;
  He looked at the maidens three ;
" I have lost my wits, you see," he said ;
  " I have lost my wits," said he.

Each maid bowed low as he gazed at her,
  In the sweet, old-fashioned way ;
For they guessed that he was a minister
  From the Massachusetts Bay.

(And one was Patience, so tall and fair ;
  And one was queenly Prue ;
And one was Hope with golden hair ;
  And the eyes of all were blue.)

He looked above and he looked around ;
  With fear their bosoms beat ;
He looked till the lifeless bird he found,
  And he lifted it by its feet.

He lifted it in his tender hands ;
  He nursed it on his breast ;
" Oh God ! " he groaned, " in what strange
    lands
  Does my own dear birdling rest ! "

He sang to the bird a thin, old tune ;
  It quavered like a rill
That, leaping the leafy steps of June,
  Goes purling at its will.

He smoothed the feathers upon its neck
  With his fingers pale and fine :
" She was white as thee, thou snowy wreck,
  But her fate is worse than thine ! "

And then he wept like a silly child,
  And the maidens wept around ;
For they doubted his wits had wandered wild
  And his heart had a cruel wound.

" Prythee tell thy tale "—the voice was
        Guye's—
  " If thou hast tale to tell ; "
The Puritan brushed his blinded eyes,
  And the maidens hearkened well.

They leaned to list to the tale accursed ;
  He leaned to their eyes, and said :
" I think, 'twas a little hair at first,—
  A hair from her lover's head !

" It came in a gift of mignonette,
  And many a dainty bloom
Of briar and pink and violet,
  Whose perfume filled her room.

" She nourished it under the nightly dew,
  She fed it from her soul ;
And it grew and grew, until she knew
  That a viper was in the bowl !

" She nourished it through the evening
  hours ;
She watched it day by day ;
She nourished it till the withered flowers
  Were culled and thrown away.

" She cherished it with a tender smile ;
  She touched it without fear ;
And I marvelled much that a thing so vile
  Should be to her so dear.

" ' Oh Hester, Hester ! my daughter sweet !
  The viper will work you harm ! '
But she trod my warning beneath her feet,
  And courted the awful charm.

" ' Oh father, father ! I may not scorn
  A creature that love hath made ;
For never was life so sweetly born,
  And I cannot be afraid.

" ' Oh, look at its glittering eyes ! ' she said ;
   ' They shine on me like stars !
And look at its dapples, so green and red,
'   And the sidelong, golden bars !

" ' Was ever a creature brave as this
   By mortal maiden found ? '
The serpent raised his head with a hiss,
   And merrily swam around !

" She laughed so loud, so long she laughed,
   That I could nought but groan ;
For I knew my child was going daft
   With the charm about her thrown.

" The bowl was strait for the noisome thing,
   And it lengthened more and more,
Till it leaped, and lay in a mottled ring
   Upon her chamber floor !

" All wonderful hues the rainbow knows
  Gleamed forth from its scaly skin,
And up from the centre its crest arose,
  And the tongue shot out and in !

"The moon was shining : I could not sleep :
  I clomb the silent stairs :
I sought her door in the midnight deep,
  And I caught her unawares !

" Fair as a lily she lay at rest
  In a flood of the ghostly sheen ;
Fair as twin lilies her virgin breast,
  And the serpent lay between !"

Each maid rose shivering like a reed ;
  They stopped their ears with dread :
" Oh sir, thou hast lost thy wits, indeed !—
  Thou hast lost thy wits !" they said.

(And one was Patience, so tall and fair ;
 And one was queenly Prue ;
And one was Hope with the golden hair ;
 And the eyes of all were blue.)

He smote them down with a look of woe !
 " I shouted and shrieked amain !
It startled back like a bended bow,
 And slid from the counterpane !

" ' Oh Hester, Hester ! how dare you lie
 With the thing upon your breast ! '
 And I waited to hear what mad reply
 Should break from the serpent's nest !

" ' Oh father dear ! why come you here ? '—
 She did not start or scream ;
' The moon shines bright this time o' the
  year ;
 I was dreaming a pleasant dream.'

" I answered her not ; I turned around ;
  I staggered to my bed ;
And there I sank in a fearful swound,
  And lay as I were dead.

" But daily ever the monster grew,
  And lengthened hour by hour,
And lazily gloated as if it knew
  It held her in its power !

" It quivered in every golden flake,
  And grew in such degree,
That it seemed the snake which the moon-
      beams make,
  Crawling across the sea.

" A silken fillet, a cord, a rope,
  A Monster, a Thing of Doom,
It sucked the air of its life and hope,
  And crowded the tainted room.

2

" The midnight hour came round again ;
    The clock ticked like a bell ;
And I heard through all my burning brain
    The sound of a deed of hell !

" It wreathed its coils around her frame ;
    It lifted her in the air ;
And I heard the dragon as it came
    Slow creeping down the stair !

" It touched the latch, the door swung back ;
    It leaped the creaking sill ;
My head was split by a thunder-crack,
    And then the world was still !

" I could not move, I could not cry,
    But I knew my child was gone ;
Like a stone in the ground I seemed to lie,
    While the clock ticked on and on !

" Out into the night they fled away—
   Out from the gaping door—
And the morning came with another day,
   But she came nevermore !

" But I saw it once !   It reared its crest
   Where the sunset clouds were piled ;
And I swear to Christ I will travel west
   Till I kiss once more my child ! "

III.

The owl dropped out of his fainting hold,
   His head fell back aghast ;
" Ah God ! " shrieked the maidens, " thy
      tale is told,
   And we fear thy soul hath passed."

Guye lifted him in his arms amain ;
   He bore him to his bed ;
And the dear Lord eased him of his pain ;
   In the midnight he was dead !

The storm grew weary along its path,
 The room was still and warm ;
But a storm arose of fiercer wrath
 Within each maiden's form.

It burst in bitterest tears and sighs ;
 It shook them with its grief ;
They could not look in their father's eyes ;
 They could not find relief.

They left the dead in the flickering gloom
 They sought their chamber door ;
And they fearfully scanned the wintry room
 For the form their fancies bore.

They looked full long but did not find
 That monstrous form of Sin ;
(Yet a viper may lodge in a maiden's mind)
 And then they looked within.

All doubtful shapes in hiding there
    They killed in God's pure sight,
And they swept their penitent souls with
        prayer
    That wild December night.

And when they woke on the morrow morn,
    They worshipped—kneeling low—
And their souls were sweet as the day new-
        born,
    And white as the drifted snow !

And one was Patience, so tall and fair ;
    And one was queenly Prue ;
And one was Hope with the golden hair ;
    And the eyes of all were blue.

JACOB HURD'S CHILD.

I.

Who breaketh his fast so early,
  While yet he can count the stars?
And whose are the footsteps trailing through
  The dew to the pasture-bars?

He snaffleth his white-eyed gelding,
  He mounteth the saddle-tree;
And out from the skirts of Ipswich town
  All grimly rideth he.

Out from the town at sunrise,
  His stubborn fields untilled,
Rideth Jacob Hurd for a day and a night
  To see three witches killed.

For Hurd is a stalwart Christian
  Whom Satan hath ne'er enticed ;
He believeth in God and His holy word,
  And he hateth Antichrist.

The devil in awe he holdeth,
  And God with an equal fear ;
And little of Gospel and much of Law
  Make up his creed severe.

With a burning zeal for his Master,
  He fighteth with Death and Hell ;
And when a witch is brought to the rope,
  It pleaseth old Jacob well.

So out of the town at sunrise,
  His stubborn fields untilled,
He rideth forth for a day and a night
  To see three witches killed.

He glanceth backward at Ipswich,
  Then leaneth low to pray,
For he knoweth that in the wilderness
  The savage haunts the way.

Look for thy last, old Jacob !
  And pray, though thy prayer be vain ;
Thy errand hath not the smile of God ;
  Thou comest not again !

II.

It is four o'clock of the evening,
  And, dressed in her hodden gray,
Old Jacob's wife is humming a tune,
  For the goodman is away.

And forth from their distant cabins
  (None see them so soon as she),
The women who hold old Hurd in fear
  Are coming to drink her tea.

There's the pretty wife of Dunster,
   With Goffe's from the meadow farm,
And the Sparhawke girls, with goodwife
   Gill,
   And the Glovers, arm in arm.

There is Peter Flynt's young widow,
   And her sister, in Lon'on brown,
And Miriam Winship : oh, sweet and wise
   Is the school-ma'am of the town !

And the heart of the goodwife, waiting
   The coming of friendly feet,
Is smitten through by an olden pang
   That is bitter at once, and sweet.

For the school-ma'am once taught him let-
   ters—
   The wonderful boy who died,
And who took from her motherly bosom all
   Its solace and its pride ;—

And Miriam's coming would surely
  Bring to her heart the joy
Of speaking, with none to make afraid,
  About her perished boy.

(For Jacob held hard to silence,
  Though he was more than sad,
And would not speak of their cruel loss
  With the mother of the lad.)

She meeteth them at her door-way
  With a greeting of hand to hand,
But she kisseth Miriam on her cheek,
  And the women understand.

III.

It is six o'clock of the evening,
  And, grouped at the table rude,
The women have bent their heads to say
  Their word of gratitude.

Now the tea and the feast are passing,
  While they gossip of home affairs—
Of the deacon's cattle in the pound,
  Or a sick child up for prayers ;—

Of a work of grace in the village,
  And the devil's work abroad,
And the mischievous witches soon to go
  To the judgment-bar of God.

But Miriam speaketh a sentence
  That winneth the ears of all,
When she turneth her eyes on good-wife
    Hurd,
  And biddeth her talk of Paul.

Tears fill the eyes of the mother,
  And the kindly women list ;
" The lips," said she, " should be good and
    wise
  That an angel's lips have kissed ;

" But in truth my lips are neither ;
    For God, by the hand of pain,
   Sent a gift that my soul misunderstood,
    And he took it back again.

" For Jacob and I had prayed him
    That who should be born of me
   Should be sanctified at his birth, and
      strong
    In the power of prophecy.

" And the prayer was sweetly answered,
    But the prophet, all unguessed,
   Grew weary of our clumsy ways,
    And entered into rest.

" It was better that he left us,
    For Jacob could not know,
   That a child's sweet story was not a lie
    To be punished by a blow.

" For he was not made like others,
  His thoughts were weird and wild ;
And Jacob at last believed, in truth,
  That a devil possessed the child.

" With the birds that gathered about him,
  He prattled for hours and hours ;
He sang to the spider upon his web,
  And the bees in the hearts of flowers.

" He carried a curious wisdom ;
  And many were the times
When he sat in the sun the livelong day,
  And sang to himself in rhymes.

" And he told such marvellous stories
  Of what he heard in the air,—
Of the talk of the birds, and the songs of
    the sea,—
  That we were in despair.

" And Jacob exclaimed : ' God help us !
    For how is a man to know
  Whether a poet comes down from heaven,
    Or climbs from the world below ? '

" One day, in the early autumn,
    When pigeons were in the woods,
  And out in the stubble the stripéd quail
    Were leading their pretty broods ;

" When the partridge drummed in the dis-
        tance,
    And the squirrel barked from the oak,
  And forth from the smoky hill-side came
    The woodman's lazy stroke,

" He went away toward the forest,
    And I saw his face no more
  Till, flushed by the red of the setting sun,
    He stood in the cabin door.

" ' Now where hast thou been ? ' said Jacob.
  ' I have been on my horse,' said he ;
And Jacob grew pale, and shook like a leaf
  As he took the lad on his knee.

" ' What horse hast thou ridden ? ' said Jacob.
  ' I have ridden my own,' he said—
  ' My golden horse with a silver tail,
  And a mane of silver thread.

" ' He came to me in the pasture,
  And he knelt for me to mount ;
And his saddle and bridle were blazing
    with
  More jewels than I could count.

" ' And he bore me like the lightning,
  Over sea and over land,
And he coursed the shore, or mounted the
    air,
  Or stopped at my command.

" ' I have seen the windy ocean,
   And flown above its waves,
And I've seen the great leviathan
   Playing within its caves.

" ' I have ridden through old England,
   Over hills and over dells,
I have cantered through the London
   streets,
   And heard the London bells.

" ' I have been to the holy places,
   And knelt and prayed in them,
And fed my golden horse with bread
   In the streets of Jerusalem.

" ' I have ridden by mighty rivers,
   From the mountains to the sea ;
And hark ! ' said he, ' for my golden horse
   Is whinnying low for me ! '

" ' Get down ! ' said Jacob, fiercely ;
   ' Thou knowest thou hast lied ;
  Surely the devil possesseth thee ! '
   And he smote him from his side.

" The sweet romancer staggered
   Into my waiting arms,
  And I kissed his cheeks without a fear
   Of Satan or his charms.

" That night he lay in a fever,
   And raved of his golden horse ;
  And Jacob sat and watched by him,
   In a helpless, dumb remorse.

" But my soul was in rebellion,
   For how could a child of prayer,
  With the love of his mother in his heart,
   Be taken in such a snare ?

3

" ' Thou believest that Mother Sewall
    Rideth a broom,' said I ;
  ' But thy darling talks of his golden horse,
    And thou smitest him for a lie.

" ' And I think, of the two, thou sinnest
    Against thy God the most ;
  For I judge thou chargest the Evil One
    With the work of the Holy Ghost ! '

" But I begged my husband's pardon,
    For he was sore distraught ;
  And would never leave the darling's bed,
    Though often I besought.

" Long days and nights thereafter,
    In his dream the sweet lad lay,
  But his fancy was on its journeying,
    And always far away.

" And he spoke of wondrous countries
 Through which his journey led,
On his golden horse with the silver tail,
 And the mane of silver thread.

" Till Jacob and I believed him,
 And would not have marvelled much
Had the golden creature revealed himself
 To our credulous sight and touch.

" But weaker he grew and weaker,
 Until there came in his eye
A look so weary and worn, we knew
 Our little boy would die.

" One still and cloudy midnight
 He woke and gazed around,
And said that he heard his golden horse
 Pawing the pasture-ground.

"I think 'twas a bolt of thunder
    Shot by a distant shower,
  That shook the earth and the window-sash
    In the last throe of its power.

"And I think it was the lightning,
    That cheated our straining eyes;
  But it seemed as if a beauteous horse
    Entered in golden guise,

"Breathing a flame from his nostrils,
    And pausing by the bed;
  When the child sprang up with a cry of
      joy,
    And sank on his pillow, dead.

"And then, on the second morning,
    We bore him to the grave,—
  The child that we were unfit to keep,
    And had no power to save.

" But in the long procession,
    No eyes but ours could see
The wondrous figure we beheld
    Leading the company.

" For following hard the neighbors
    Who bore the precious corse,
Rode little Paul right gallantly
    Upon his golden horse.

" I saw him just as plainly
    As e'er I saw a flame ;
And he nodded to me with a smile,
    And Jacob saw the same."

IV.

The story and feast are ended,
    And forth from the open door,
With eyelids wide and faces flushed,
    The guests of the evening pour.

The sun in the west is setting,
  And bathing each farm and fold
With the lifted dust of the village ways
  In an atmosphere of gold.

Now what is that in the distance
  Which catches each gazing eye ?
'Tis a flurry of dust that travels fast,
  Like a whirlwind from the sky !

Nearer it comes, and nearer,
  Till all the gazers know
That a horse is running without a man
  Behind the saddle-bow !

He courses along the highway
  That leads across the plain,
And they hear the beat of his heavy feet
  As he rushes down the lane.

And, leaning on Miriam Winship,
  A cry in her frightened breath,
The goodwife Hurd knows well that the
    horse
  Is the messenger of death ;

And that somewhere among the shadows
  Her husband lies apart,
With the scalp-lock riven from his head
  And an arrow in his heart.

And the women scream in wonder,
  For all can plainly see
That a little lad with a smiling face
  Bestrides the saddle-tree.

He tosses a kiss to his mother,
  He tenderly bows to all,
And they know that their eyes behold in-
    deed,
  The spirit of little Paul.

The horse flies by the cottage,
  And into his pasture home,
Yellow and bright in the sunset gold,
  And spotted with silver foam.

And the women hasten homeward,
  Among the dropping dews,
To tell of the marvels they have seen,
  And to bear the heavy news.

But Miriam passeth inward,
  Her hand in goodwife Hurd's,
And readeth there, for her comforting,
  The Bible's gracious words.

Then reverently she kneeleth
  And uttereth a prayer,
That the childless and the widowed one
  May have the Father's care.

But ere her prayer she endeth,
  With fervent voice she saith :
" Oh punish not our blundering more
  With chastisement of death !

" But when thou sendest poets
  To such dull folk as we,
Inspire our blind and doubting eyes
  To know them when we see ! "

THE PALMER'S VISION.

NOON o'er Judea! All the air was beating
With the hot pulses of the day's great heart;
The birds were silent, and the rill retreating
Shrank in its covert, and complained apart,

When a lone pilgrim, with his scrip and bur-
    don,
Dropped by the wayside, weary and dis-
    tressed,
His sinking heart grown faithless of its guer-
    don—
The city of his recompense and rest.

No vision yet of Galilee and Tabor!
No glimpse of distant Zion throned and
    crowned!
Behind him stretched his long and useless
    labor,
Before him lay the parched and stony ground.

He leaned against a shrine of Mary, casting
Its balm of shadow on his aching head,
And worn with toil, and faint with cruel fast-
    ing,
He sighed : " O God ! O God, that I were
    dead !

" The friends I loved are lost or left behind
    me ;
In penury and loneliness I roam ;
These endless paths of penance choke and
    blind me ;
Oh come and take thy wasted pilgrim home!"

Then with the form of Mary bending o'er him,
Her hands in changeless benediction stayed,
The palmer slept, while a swift dream upbore
    him
To the fair paradise for which he prayed.

He stood alone, wrapped in divinest wonder ;
He saw the pearly gates and jasper walls
Informed with light, and heard the far-off
    thunder
Of chariot wheels and mighty waterfalls !

From far and near, in rhythmic palpitations,
Rose on the air the noise of shouts and
    psalms ;
And through the gates he saw the ransomed
    nations,
Marching and waving their triumphant palms.

And white within the thronging Empyrean,
A golden palm-branch in his kingly hand,
He saw his Lord, the gracious Galilean,
Amid the worship of his myriads stand !

" O Jesus ! Lord of glory ! Bid me enter !
I worship thee ! I kiss thy holy rood ! "
The pilgrim cried, when from the burning
    centre
A broad-winged angel sought him where he
    stood.

" Why art thou here ? " in accents deep and
    tender
Outspoke the messenger. "Dost thou not
    know
That none may win the city's rest and splen-
    dor,
Who do not cut their palms in Jericho ?

"Go back to earth, thou palmer empty-
  handed !
Go back to hunger and the toilsome way !
Complete the task that duty hath com-
  manded,
And win the palm thou hast not brought to-
  day ! "

And then the sleeper woke, and gazed
  around him ;
Then springing to his feet with life renewed,
He spurned the faithless weakness that had
  bound him,
And, faring on, his pilgrimage pursued.

The way was hard, and he grew halt and
  weary,
But one long day, among the evening hours,
He saw beyond a landscape gray and dreary
The sunset flame on Salem's sacred towers !

O, fainting soul that readest well this story,
Longing through pain for death's benignant
  balm,
Think not to win a heaven of rest and glory
If thou shalt reach its gates without thy palm !

TO WHITTIER ON HIS SEVEN-
TIETH BIRTHDAY.

TEN gentle-hearted boys of seven,
Too young and sweet to stray from heaven,
Will—counting up the little men—
Amount to three score years and ten.

Two gracious men of thirty-five,
With wits alert and hearts alive,
Will fill complete the rounded spheres
Of seventy strong and manly years.

Nay, Whittier, thou art not old ;
Thy register a lie hath told,
For lives devote to love and truth
Do only multiply their youth.

Thou art ten gentle boys of seven,
With souls too sweet to stray from heaven ;
Thou art two men of thirty-five,
With wits alert, and hearts alive !

A GLIMPSE OF YOUTH.

MAIDEN, I thank thee for thy face,
Thy sweet, shy glance of conscious eyes ;
For, from thy beauty and thy grace,
My life has won a glad surprise.

I met thee on the crowded street—
A load of care on heart and brain—
And, for a moment, bright and fleet,
The vision made me young again.

And then I thought, as on I went,
And struggled through the thronging ways,
How every age's complement
The age that follows overlays.

The youth upon the child shuts down ;
Young manhood closes over youth ;
And ripe old age is but the crown
That keeps them both in changeless truth !

So, every little child I see,
With brow and spirit undefiled,
And simple faith and frolic glee,
Finds still in me another child.

Toward every brave and careless boy
Whose lusty shout or call I hear,
The boy within me springs with joy
And rings an echo to his cheer !

What was it, when thy face I saw,
That moved my spirit like a breeze,
Responsive to the primal law
Of youth's entrancing harmonies ?

4

Ah ! little maid—so sweet and shy—
Building each day thy fair romance—
Thou didst not dream a youth passed by,
When I returned thee glance for glance !

For all my youth is still my own,—
Bound in the volume of my age,—
And breath from thee hath only blown
The leaves back to the golden page !

THE MARBLE PROPHECY.

The harlequins are out in force to-day—
The piebald Swiss—and in the vestibule
Of great St. Peter's rings the rhythmic tread
Of Roman nobles, uniformed and armed
As the Pope's Guard ; and while their double
    line
With faultless curve enters the open door,
And sways and sparkles up the splendid
    nave,
Between the walls of humbler soldiery,
And parts to pass the altar—keeping step
To the proud beating of their Roman
    hearts—
A breeze of whispered admiration sweeps
The crowds that gaze, and dies within the
    dome.

St. Peter's toe (the stump of it) was cold
An hour ago, but waxes warm apace
With rub of handkerchiefs, and dainty touch
Of lips and foreheads.

　　　　　　　　　　Smug behind their screen
Sit the Pope's Choir. No woman enters
　　　there ;
For woman is impure, and makes impure
By voice and presence ! Mary, mother of
　　　God !
Not thy own sex may sing thee in the
　　　courts
Of The All-Holy !—Only man, pure man !
Doubt not the purity of some of these—
Angels before their time—nor doubt
That they will sing like angels, when
　　　Papa,
Borne on the shoulders of his stalwart men
(The master rode an ass), and canopied
By golden tapestries—the triple crown

Upon his brow, the nodding peacock plumes
Far heralding his way—shall come to take
His incense and his homage.

                            I will go.
'Tis a brave pageant, to be seen just
    once.
'Tis a brave pageant, but one does not
    like
To smutch his trousers kneeling to a man,
Or bide the stare that follows if he fail:
So, having seen it once, one needs not
    wait.

What is the feast? Let's see: ah! I re-
    call:
St. Peter's chair was brought from An-
    tioch
So many years ago;—the worse for wear
No doubt, and never quite luxurious,

But valued as a piece of furniture
By Rome above all price; and so they
    give
High honor to the anniversary.
'Tis well; in Rome they make account
    of chairs.
If less in heaven, it possibly may be
Because they're greatly occupied by joy
Over bad men made penitent and pure
By this same chair! Who knows?

                    I'll to the door!
The sun seems kind and simple in the sky
After such pomp. I thank thee, Sun!
    Thou hast
A smile like God, that reaches to the
    heart
Direct and sweet, without the ministries
Of scene and ceremonial! Thy rays
Fall not in benediction at the ends

Of two pale fingers; but thy warmth and
    light
Wrap well the cold dark world.   I need
    no prism
To teach my soul that thou art beautiful:
It would divide thee, and confuse my sight.
Shine freely, sun !   No mighty mother
    church
Stands mediator between thee and me!
Ay, shine on these—all these in shivering
    need—
To whom God's precious love is doled or
    sold
By sacerdotal hucksters!   Shine on these,
And teach them that the God of Life
    and Light
Dwells not alone in temples made by
    hands ;
And that the path to Him, from every
    soul,
In every farthest corner of the earth,
Is as direct as are thy rays to thee !

Ha! Pardon! Have I hurt you? Wella-
    day!
I was not looking for a beggar here:—
Indeed, was looking upward! But I see
You're here by royal license—with a badge
Made of good brass. Come nearer to me!
    there:
Take double alms, and give me chance to
    read
The number on your breast. So: "Sev-
    enty-seven"!
'Tis a good number, man, and quite at
    home
About the temple. Well, you have hard
    fare,
But many brothers and no end of shows!
Think it not ill that they will spend to-
    day,
Touching this chair, enough of time and
    gold
To gorge the poor of Rome. The men
    who hold

The church in charge—who are, indeed,
    the church—
Have little time to give to starving men.
Be thankful for your label! Only one
Can be the beggar "Number seventy-
    seven"!
They are distinguished persons: so are you!
You must be patient, though it seems, I
    grant,
A trifle odd that when a miracle
Is wrought before you, it will never take
A useful turn, as in the olden time,
And give you loaves and fishes, or in-
    crease
Your little dinners!

               Still the expectant crowds
Press up the street from round St. Angelo,
And thread the circling colonnade, or cross
With hurried steps the broad piazza—
    crowds

That pass the portal, and at once are lost
Within the vaulted glooms, as morning mist
Is quenched by morning air.

It is God's house—
The noblest temple ever reared to Him
By hands of men—the culminating deed
Of a great church—the topmost reach of
      art
For the enshrinement of the Christian faith
In sign and symbol. Holiness becomes
The temple of the Holy!

And these crowds?
Come they to pour the worship of their
      hearts
Like wine upon the altar? Who are they?
Last night, we hear, the theatre was full.
It was a spectacle: they went to see.

All yesterday they thronged the galleries,
Or roved among the ruins, or drove out
Upon the broad campagna—just to see.
This afternoon, with gaudy equipage,
(Their Bædeker and Murray left at home),
They'll be upon the Pincio—to see.
And so this morning, learning of the chair
And the Pope's coming, they are here to see
(The men in swallow-tails, their wives in
    black),
The grandest spectacle of all the week.
Make way ye men of poverty and dirt
Who fringe the outer lines! Make open-
    way
And let them pass! This is the House of
    God,
And swallow-tails are of fine moment here!

The ceremony has begun within.
I hear the far, faint voices of the choir,

As if a door in heaven were left ajar,
And cherubim were singing ... Now I hear
The sharp, metallic chink of grounded arms
Upon the marble, as His Holiness
Moves up the lines of bristling bayonets
That guard his progress. . . . But I stay
    alone.
Nay, I will to the Vatican, and there,
In converse with the thoughts of manlier
    men,
Pass the great morning! I shall be alone—
Ay, all alone with thee, Laocöon!

"A feast day and no entrance"? Can
    one's gold
Unloose a soul from purgatorial bonds
And ope the gates of heaven, without the
    power
To draw a bolt at the Museum? Wait!

Laocöon! thou great embodiment
Of human life and human history!
Thou record of the past, thou prophecy
Of the sad future, thou majestic voice,
Pealing along the ages from old time!
Thou wail of agonized humanity!
There lives no thought in marble like to
    thee!
Thou hast no kindred in the Vatican,
But standest separate among the dreams
Of old mythologies—alone—alone!
The beautiful Apollo at thy side
Is but a marble dream, and dreams are all
The gods and goddesses and fauns and fates
That populate these wondrous halls; but
    thou,
Standing among them, liftest up thyself
In majesty of meaning, till they sink
Far from the sight, no more significant
Than the poor toys of children. For thou
    art
A voice from out the world's experience,

Speaking of all the generations past
To all the generations yet to come
Of the long struggle, the sublime despair,
The wild and weary agony of man!

Ay, Adam and his offspring, in the toils
Of the twin serpents Sin and Suffering,
Thou dost impersonate ; and as I gaze
Upon the twining monsters that enfold
In unrelaxing, unrelenting coils,
Thy awful energies, and plant their fangs
Deep in thy quivering flesh, while still thy
        might
In fierce convulsion foils the fateful wrench
That would destroy thee, I am overwhelmed
With a strange sympathy of kindred
        pain,
And see through gathering tears the tragedy,
The curse and conflict of a ruined race !

Those Rhodian sculptors were gigantic men,
Whose inspirations came from other source
Than their religion, though they chose to
    speak
Through its familiar language,—men who
    saw,
And, seeing quite divinely, felt how weak
To cure the world's great woe were all
    the powers
Whose reign their age acknowledged. So
    they sat—
The immortal three—and pondered long and
    well
What one great work should speak the
    truth for them,—
What one great work should rise and testify
That they had found the topmost fact of
    life,
Above the reach of all philosophies
And all religions—every scheme of man
To placate or dethrone. That fact they
    found,

And moulded into form.   The silly priest
Whose desecrations of the altar stirred
The vengeance of his God, and summoned
      forth
The wreathed gorgons of the slimy deep
To crush him and his children, was the word
By which they spoke to their own age and
      race,
That listened and applauded, knowing not
That high above the small significance
They apprehended, rose the grand intent
That mourned their doom and breathed a
      world's despair!

Be sure it was no fable that inspired
So grand an utterance.   Perchance some leaf
From an old Hebrew record had conveyed
A knowledge of the genesis of man.
Perchance some fine conception rose in them
Of unity of nature and of race,

Springing from one beginning. Nay, per-
    chance
Some vision flashed before their thoughtful
    eyes
Inspired by God, which showed the mighty
    man,
Who, unbegotten, had begot a race
That to his lot was linked through count-
    less time
By living chains, from which in vain it strove
To wrest its tortured limbs and leap amain
To freedom and to rest! It matters not:
The double word—the fable and the fact,
The childish figment and the mighty truth,
Are blent in one. The first was for a day
And dying Rome; the last for later time
And all mankind.

       These sculptors spoke their word
And then they died; and Rome—imperial
    Rome—

The mistress of the world—debauched by
    blood
And foul with harlotries—fell prone at length
Among the trophies of her crimes and slept.
Down toppling one by one her helpless gods
Fell to the earth, and hid their shattered
    forms
Within the dust that bore them, and among
The ruined shrines and crumbling masonry
Of their old temples. Still this wondrous
    group,
From its long home upon the Esquiline,
Beheld the centuries of change, and stood,
Impersonating in its conscious stone
The unavailing struggle to crowd back
The closing folds of doom. It paused to
    hear
A strange New Name proclaimed among
    the streets,
And catch the dying shrieks of martyred
    men,
And see the light of hope and heroism

Kindling in many eyes; and then it fell;
And in the ashes of an empire swathed
Its aching sense, and hid its tortured forms.

The old life went, the new life came; and
    Rome
That slew the prophets built their sepul-
    chres,
And filled her heathen temples with the
    shrines
Of Christian saints whom she had tossed
    to beasts,
Or crucified, or left to die in chains
Within her dungeons. Ay, the old life
    went
But came again. The primitive, true age—
The simple, earnest age—when Jesus Christ
The Crucified was only known and preached,
Struck hands with paganism and passed
    away.

Rome built new temples and installed new
    names ;
Set up her graven images, and gave
To Pope and priests the keeping of her gods.
Again she grasped at power no longer hers
By right of Roman prowess, and stretched
    out
Her hand upon the consciences of men.
The godlike liberty with which the Christ
Had made his people free she stole from them,
And bound them slaves to new observances.
Her times, her days, her ceremonials
Imposed a burden grievous to be borne,
And millions groaned beneath it. Nay, she
    grew
The vengeful persecutor of the free
Who would not bear her yoke, and bathed
    her hands
In blood as sweet as ever burst from hearts
Torn from the bosoms of the early saints
Within her Coliseum. She assumed
To be the arbiter of destiny.

Those whom she bound or loosed upon the
    earth,
Were bound or loosed in heaven! In God's
    own place,
She sat as God—supreme, infallible!
She shut the door of knowledge to man-
    kind,
And bound the Word Divine. She sucked
    the juice
Of all prosperities within her realms,
Until her gaudy temples blazed with gold,
And from a thousand altars flashed the fire
Of priceless gems. To win her countless
    wealth
She sold as merchandise the gift of God.
She took the burden which the cross had
    borne,
And bound it fast to scourged and writh-
    ing loins
In thriftless Penance, till her devotees
Fled from their kind to find the boon of
    peace,

And died in banishment. Beneath her sway,
The proud old Roman blood grew thin and
    mean
Till virtue was the name it gave to fear,
Till heroism and brigandage were one,
And neither slaves nor beggars knew their
    shame!

What marvel that a shadow fell, world-wide,
And brooded o'er the ages? Was it strange
That in those dim and drowsy centuries,
When the dumb earth had ceased to quake
    beneath
The sounding wheels of progress, and the
    life
That erst had flamed so high had sunk so
    low
In cold monastic glooms and forms as cold,
The buried gods should listen in their sleep
And dream of resurrection? Was it strange

That listening well they should at length
    awake,
And struggle from their pillows? Was it
    strange
That men whose vision grovelled should
    perceive
The dust in motion, and with rapture greet
Each ancient deity with loud acclaim,
As if he brought with him the good old
    days
Of manly art and poetry and power?
Nay, was it strange that as they raised them-
    selves,
And cleaned their drowsy eyelids of the dust,
And took their godlike attitudes again,
The grand old forms should feel themselves
    at home—
Saving perhaps a painful sense that men
Had dwindled somewhat? Was it strange,
    at last,
That all these gods should be installed anew,
And share the palace with His Holiness,

And that the Pope and Christian Rome can
    show
No art that equals that which had its birth
In pagan inspiration? Ah, what shame!
That after two millenniums of Christ,
Rome calls to her the thirsty tribes of earth,
And smites the heathen marble with her rod,
And bids them drink the best she has to
    give!

And when the gods were on their feet again
It was thy time to rise, Laocöon!
Those Rhodian sculptors had foreseen it all.
Their word was true: thou hadst the right
    to live.

In the quick sunlight on the Esquiline,
Where thou didst sleep, De Fredis kept his
    vines;

And long above thee grew the grapes whose
    blood
Ran wild in Christian arteries, and fed
The fire of Christian revels. Ah what fruit
Sucked up the marrow of thy marble there!
What fierce, mad dreams were those that
    scared the souls
Of men who drank, nor guessed what ichor
    stung
Their crimson lips, and tingled in their veins!
Strange growths were those that sprang
    above thy sleep:
Vines that were serpents; huge and ugly
    trunks
That took the forms of human agony—
Contorted, gnarled and grim—and leaves
    that bore
The semblance of a thousand tortured hands,
And snaky tendrils that entwined them-
    selves
Around all forms of life within their reach.
And crushed or blighted them!

                        At last the spade
Slid down to find the secret of the vines,
And touched thee with a thrill that startled
        Rome,
And swiftly called a shouting multitude
To witness thy unveiling.

                        Ah what joy
Greeted the rising from thy long repose!
And one, the mighty master of his time,
The king of Christian art, with strong,
        sad face
Looked on, and wondered with the giddy
        crowd,—
Looked on and learned (too late, alas! for
        him),
That his humanity and God's own truth
Were more than Christian Rome, and spoke
        in words
Of larger import. Humbled Angelo
Bowed to the masters of the early days,

Grasped their strong hands across the
    centuries,
And went his way despairing !

               Thou, meantime,
Dids't find thyself installed among the gods
Here in the Vatican; and thou, to-day,
Hast the same word for those who read thee
    well
As when thou wast created. Rome has
    failed :
Humanity is writhing in the toils
Of the old monsters as it writhed of old,
And there is neither help nor hope in her.
Her priests, her shrines, her rites, her
    mummeries,
Her pictures and her pageants, are as weak
To break the hold of Sin and Suffering
As those her reign displaced. Her iron
    hand

Shrivels the manhood it presumes to bless
Drives to disgust or infidelity
The strong and free who dare to think and
    judge,
And wins a kiss from coward lips alone.
She does not preach the Gospel to the poor,
But takes it from their hands. The men
    who tread
The footsteps of the Master, and bow down
Alone to Him, she brands as heretics
Or hunts as fiends. She drives beyond her
    gates
The Christian worshippers of other climes,
And other folds and faiths, as if their brows
Were white with leprosy, and grants them
    there
With haughty scorn the privilege to kneel
In humble worship of the common Lord!

Is this the Christ, or look we still for Him?
Is the old problem solved, or lingers yet

The grand solution? Ay Laocöon!
Thy word is true, for Christian Rome has
    failed,
And I behold humanity in thee
As those who shaped thee saw it, when
    old Rome
In that far pagan evening fell asleep.

THE WINGS.

A feeble wail was heard at night,
  And a stifled cry of joy;
And when the morn broke cool and light,
They bore to the mother's tearful sight
  A fair and lovely boy.

Months passed away;
And day by day
  The mother hung about her child
As in his little cot he lay,
  And watched him as he smiled,
And threw his hands into the air,
  And turned above his large, bright eyes,
With an expression half of prayer
And half of strange surprise;
    For hovering o'er his downy head

A dainty vision hung.
 Fluttering, swaying,
Unsteadily it swung,
  As if suspended by a thread,
 His own sweet breath obeying.

Sometimes with look of wild beseeching
 He marked it as it dropped
Almost within his awkward reaching,
And as the vision stopped
 Beyond his anxious grasp,
 And cheated the quick clasp
Of dimpled hands, and quite
Smothered his chirrup of delight,
 And he saw his effort vain
 And the bright vision there again
Dancing before his sight,
  His eyes grew dim with tears,
  Till o'er the flooded spheres
   The soothing eye-lids crept,
   And the tired infant slept.

He saw—his mother could not see—
A presence and a mystery:
   Two waving wings,
Spangled with silver, starlike things:
   No form of light was borne between;
   Only the wings were seen!

Years steal away with silent feet,
   And he, the little one,
With brow more fair and voice more sweet
   Is playing in the sun.
Flowers are around him and the songs
   Of bounding streams and happy birds,
But sweeter than their sweetest tongues
   Break forth his own glad words.
      And as he sings
      The wings, the wings!
    Before him still they fly!
And nothing that the summer brings
    Can so entice his eye.
   Hovering here, hovering there,
    Hovering everywhere,

They flash and shine among the flowers,
While dripping sheen in golden showers
Falls through the air where'er they hover
Upon the radiant things they cover.
Hurrying here, hurrying there,
Hurrying everywhere,
He plucks the flowers they shine upon,
But while he plucks their light is gone!
And casting down the faded things,
Onward he springs
To follow the wings!

Years run away with silent feet;
The boy, to manhood grown,
Within a shadowy retreat
Stands anxious and alone.
His bosom heaves with heavy sighs,
His hair hangs damp and long,
But fiery purpose fills his eyes,
And his limbs are large and strong:
And there above a gentle hill,

The wings are hovering still,
While their soft radiance, rich and warm,
Falls on a maiden's form.

And see! again he starts,
And onward darts,
Then pauses with a fierce and sudden pain,
Then presses on again,
Till with mixed thoughts of rapture and
despair,
He kneels before her there:—
With hands together prest,
He prays to her with low and passionate calls,
And, like a snow-flake pure, she flutters, falls,
And melts upon his breast.

Long in that dearest trance he hung--
Then raised his eyes; the wings that swung
In glancing circles round his head

Afar had fled,
And wheeled, with calm and graceful flight,
Over a scene
That glowed with glories beauteously bright
Beneath their sheen.

High in the midst a monument arose,
Of pale enduring marble; calm and still,
It seemed a statue of sublime repose,
The silent speaker of a mighty will.

Its sides were hung around
With boughs of evergreen; and its long
shaft was crowned
With a bright laurel-wreath,
And glittering beneath
Were piled great heaps of gold upon the
ground.
Children were playing near—fair boys and
girls,

Who shook their sunny curls,
And laughed and sang in mirthfulness of
　　spirit,
　　And in their childish pleasures
　　Danced around the treasures
Of gold and honor they were to in-
　　herit.

The sight has fired his brain;
Onward he springs again.
　　O'er ruined blocks
Of wild and perilous rocks,
Through long damp caves, o'er pitfalls
　　dire,
And maddening scenes of blood and fire,
　　Fainting with heat,
　　Benumbed with cold,
　　With weary, aching feet,
　　He sternly toils, and presses on to
　　greet
The monument, the laurels and the gold.

Years have passed by; a shattered form
    Leans faintly on a monument;
    His glazing eyes are bent
In sadness down: a tear falls to the ground
That through the furrows of his cheek hath
    wound.
The children beautiful have ceased to play,
Tarnished the marble stands with dark
    decay,
The laurels all are dead, and flown the gold
    away

Once more he raised his eyes; before
    him lay
    A dim and lonely vale,
And feebly tottering in the downward
    way
    Walked spectres cold and pale.
And darkling groves of shadowy cypress
    sprung

Among the damp clouds that around them
    hung.
  One vision only cheers his aching sight;
    Those wings of light
Have lost their varied hues, and changed to
    white,
  And, with a gentle motion, slowly wave
    Over a new made grave.
He casts one faltering, farewell look behind,
Around, above, one mournful glance he
    throws,
Then with a cheerful smile, and trusting
    mind,
Moves feebly toward the valley of repose.
He stands above the grave; dull shudders
    creep
Along his limbs, cold drops are on his brow;
One sigh he heaves, and sinking into sleep
He drops and disappears;—and dropping
    now,
  The wings have followed too.
  But, lo! new visions burst upon the view!

They reappear in glory bright and new!
And to their sweet embrace a soul is given,
And on the wings of HOPE an angel flies
    to HEAVEN.

INTIMATIONS.

WHAT glory then! What darkness now!
  A glimpse, a thrill, and it is flown!
  I reach, I grasp, but stand alone,
With empty arms and upward brow!

Ye may not see, O weary eyes!
  The band of angels, swift and bright,
  That pass, but cannot wake your sight,
Down trooping from the crowded skies.

O heavy ears! Ye may not hear
  The strains that pass my conscious soul,
  And seek, but find no earthly goal,
Far falling from another sphere.

Ah! soul of mine! Ah! soul of mine!
  Thy sluggish senses are but bars
  That stand between thee and the stars,
And shut thee from the world divine.

For something sweeter far than sound,
  And something finer than the light
  Comes through the discord and the night
And penetrates, or wraps thee round.

Nay, God is here, couldst thou but see;
  All things of beauty are of Him;
  And heaven, that holds the cherubim,
As lovingly embraces thee!

If thou hast apprehended well
  The tender glory of a flower,
  Which moved thee, by some subtle power
Whose source and sway thou couldst not tell;

If thou hast kindled to the sweep
 Of stormy clouds across the sky,
 Or gazed with tranced and tearful eye,
And swelling breast, upon the deep;

If thou hast felt the throb and thrill
 Of early day and happy birds,
 While peace, that drowned thy chosen
  words
Has flowed from thee in glad good-will,

Then hast thou drunk the heavenly dew
 Then have thy feet in rapture trod
 The pathway of a thought of God;
And death can show thee nothing new.

For heaven and beauty are the same,—
 Of God the all-informing thought,
 To sweet, supreme expression wrought
And syllabled by sound and flame.

The light that beams from childhood's eyes,
  The charm that dwells in summer woods,
  The holy influence that broods
O'er all things under twilight skies,—

The music of the simple notes
  That rise from happy human homes,
  The joy in life of all that roams
Upon the earth, and all that floats,

Proclaim that heaven's sweet providence
  Enwraps the homely earth in whole,
  And finds the secret of the soul
Through channels subtler than the sense.

O soul of mine! Throw wide thy door,
  And cleanse thy paths from doubt and sin;
  And the bright flood shall enter in
And give thee heaven forevermore!

WORDS.

The robin repeats his two musical words,
   The meadow-lark whistles his one refrain;
   And steadily, over and over again,
The same song swells from a hundred birds.

Bobolink, chickadee, blackbird and jay,
   Thrasher and woodpecker, cuckoo and
      wren,
   Each sings its word, or its phrase, and then
It has nothing further to sing or to say.

Into that word, or that sweet little phrase,
   All there may be of its life must crowd;
   And lulling and liquid, or hoarse and loud,
It breathes out its burden of joy and praise.

A little child sits in his father's door,
  Chatting and singing with careless tongue ;
  A thousand beautiful words are sung,
And he holds unuttered a thousand more.

Words measure power ; and they measure
    thine ;
  Greater art thou in thy prattling moods
  Than all the singers of all the woods ;
They are brutes only, but thou art divine.

Words measure destiny.   Power to declare
  Infinite ranges of passion and thought
  Holds with the infinite only its lot,—
Is of eternity only the heir.

Words measure life, and they measure its joy!
  Thou hast more joy in thy childish years
  Than the birds of a hundred tuneful
    spheres,
So—sing with the beautiful birds, my boy!

SLEEPING AND DREAMING.

I softly sink into the bath of sleep:
  With eyelids shut, I see around me close
The mottled, violet vapors of the deep,
  That wraps me in repose.

I float all night in the ethereal sea
  That drowns my pain and weariness in
      balm,
Careless of where its currents carry me,
  Or settle into calm.

That which the ear can hear is silent all;
  But, in the lower stillness which I reach,
Soft whispers call me, like the distant fall
  Of waves upon the beach.

Now like the mother who with patient care
  Has soothed to rest her faint, o'erwearied
      boy,
My spirit leaves the couch, and seeks the air
  For freedom and for joy.

Drunk up like vapors by the morning sun
  The past and future rise and disappear;
And times and spaces gather home, and run
  Into a common sphere.

My youth is round me, and the silent tomb
  Has burst to set its fairest prisoner free,
And I await her in the dewy gloom
  Of the old trysting tree.

I mark the flutter of her snowy dress,
  I hear the tripping of her fairy feet,
And now, pressed closely in a pure caress,
  With ardent joy we meet.

I tell again the story of my love,
  I drink again her lip's delicious wine,
And, while the same old stars look down
      above,
    Her eyes look up to mine.

I dream that I am dreaming, and I
      start ;
  Then dream that nought so real comes
      in dreams ;
Then kiss again to reassure my heart
    That she is what she seems.

Our steps tend homeward. Lingering at
      the gate,
  I breathe, and breathe again, my fond
      good night.
She shuts the cruel door, and still I
      wait
    To watch her window-light.

I see the shadow of her dainty head,
  On curtains that I pray her hand may
    stir,
Till all is dark; and then I seek my
    bed
  To dream I dream of her.

Like the swift moon that slides from cloud
    to cloud,
  With only hurried space to smile between,
I pierce the phantoms that around me
    crowd,
  And glide from scene to scene.

I clasp warm hands that long have lain in
    dust,
  I hear sweet voices that have long been
    still,
And earth and sea give up their hallowed
    trust
  In answer to my will.

And now, high-gazing toward the starry
   dome,
  I see three airy forms come floating
    down—
The long-lost angels of my early home—
  My night of joy to crown.

They pause above, beyond my eager
   reach,
  With arms enwreathed and forms of heav-
    enly grace;
And smiling back the love that smiles from
   each,
  I see them, face to face.

They breathe no language, but their holy
   eyes
  Beam an embodied blessing on my heart,
That warm within my trustful bosom
   lies,
  And never will depart.

I drink the effluence, till through all my soul
    I feel a flood of peaceful rapture flow,
That swells to joy at last, and bursts control,
    And I awake ; but lo !

With eyelids shut, I hold the vision fast.
    And still detain it by my ardent prayer,
Till faint and fainter grown, it fades at last
    Into the silent air.

My God ! I thank Thee for the bath of sleep,
    That wraps in balm my weary heart and
        brain,
And drowns within its waters still and deep
    My sorrow and my pain.

I thank Thee for my dreams, which loose
        the bond
    That binds my spirit to its daily load,
And give it angel wings, to fly beyond
    Its slumber-bound abode.

I thank Thee for these glimpses of the clime
  That lies beyond the boundaries of sense,
Where I shall wash away the stains of time
  In floods of recompense :—

Where, when this body sleeps to wake no
    more,
  My soul shall rise to everlasting dreams,
And find unreal all it saw before
  And real all that seems.

ON THE RIGHI.

On the Righi Kulm we stood,
  Lovely Floribel and I,
While the morning's crimson flood
  Streamed along the eastern sky.
Reddened every mountain peak
  Into rose, from twilight dun;
But the blush upon her cheek
  Was not lighted by the sun!

On the Righi Kulm we sat,
  Lovely Floribel and I,
Plucking blue-bells for her hat
  From a mound that blossomed nigh.
"We are near to heaven," she sighed,
  While her raven lashes fell.
"Nearer," softly I replied,
  "Than the mountain's height may tell."

Down the Righi's side we sped,
　　Lovely Floribel and I,
But her morning blush had fled,
　　And the blue-bells all were dry.
Of the height the dream was born;
　　Of the lower air it died;
And the passion of the morn
　　Flagged and fell at eventide

From the breast of blue Lucerne,
　　Lovely Floribel and I
Saw the brand of sunset burn
　　On the Righi Kulm, and die.
And we wondered, gazing thus,
　　If our dream would still remain
On the height, and wait for us
　　Till we climb to heaven again!

GRADATIM.

HEAVEN is not reached at a single bound,
  But we build the ladder by which we rise
  From the lowly earth to the vaulted skies,
And we mount to its summit round by
    round.

I count this thing to be grandly true:
  That a noble deed is a step toward God,—
  Lifting the soul from the common clod
To a purer air and a broader view.

We rise by the things that are under feet;
  By what we have mastered of good and
    gain;
  By the pride deposed and the passion slain,
And the vanquished ills that we hourly
    meet.

We hope, we aspire, we resolve, we trust,
  When the morning calls us to life and
    light,
  But our hearts grow weary, and, ere the
    night,
Our lives are trailing the sordid dust.

We hope, we resolve, we aspire, we pray,
  And we think that we mount the air on
    wings
  Beyond the recall of sensual things,
While our feet still cling to the heavy
    clay.

Wings for the angels, but feet for men!
  We may borrow the wings to find the
    way—
  We may hope, and resolve, and aspire, and
    pray;
But our feet must rise, or we fall again.

Only in dreams is a ladder thrown
  From the weary earth to the sapphire
    walls ;
  But the dreams depart, and the vision
    falls,
And the sleeper wakes on his pillow of stone.

Heaven is not reached at a single bound ;
  But we build the ladder by which we rise
  From the lowly earth to the vaulted skies,
And we mount to its summit, round by
    round.

RETURNING CLOUDS.

THE clouds are returning after the rain.
  All the long morning they steadily sweep
  From the blue Northwest, o'er the upper
    main,
  In a peaceful flight to their Eastern sleep.

With sails that the cool wind fills or furls,
  And shadows that darken the billowy
    grass,
Freighted with amber or piled with pearls,
  Fleets of fair argosies rise and pass.

The earth smiles back to the smiling throng
  From greening pasture and blooming field,

For the earth that had sickened with thirst
    so long
  Has been touched by the hand of The
    Rain, and healed.

The old man sits 'neath the tall elm trees,
  And watches the pageant with dreamy
    eyes,
While his white locks stir to the same cool
    breeze
  That scatters the silver along the skies.

The old man's eyelids are wet with tears—
  Tears of sweet pleasure and sweeter
    pain—
For his thoughts are driving back over the
    years
  In beautiful clouds after life's long rain.

Sorrows that drowned all the springs of his
    life,
  Trials that crushed him with pitiless
    beat,
Storms of temptation and tempests of
    strife,
  Float o'er his memory tranquil and sweet.

And the old man's spirit, made soft and
    bright
  By the long, long rain that had bent him
    low,
Sees a vision of angels on wings of white,
  In the trooping clouds as they come and
    go.

EUREKA.

WHOM I crown with love is royal;
    Matters not her blood or birth;
She is queen, and I am loyal
    To the noblest of the earth.

Neither place, nor wealth, nor title,
    Lacks the man my friendship owns;
His distinction, true and vital,
    Shines supreme o'er crowns and thrones.

Where true love bestows its sweetness,
    Where true friendship lays its hand,
Dwells all greatness, all completeness,
    All the wealth of every land.

Man is greater than condition,
  And where man himself bestows,
He begets, and gives position
  To the gentlest that he knows.

Neither miracle nor fable
  Is the water changed to wine;
Lords and ladies at my table
  Prove Love's simplest fare divine.

And if these accept my duty,
  If the loved my homage own,
I have won all worth and beauty;
  I have found the magic stone.

WHERE SHALL THE BABY'S DIMPLE BE?

OVER the cradle the mother hung,
  Softly crooning a slumber-song;
And these were the simple words she sung
  All the evening long:

"Cheek or chin, or knuckle or knee,
Where shall the baby's dimple be?
Where shall the angel's finger rest
When he comes down to the baby's nest?
Where shall the angel's touch remain
When he awakens my babe again?"

Still as she bent and sang so low,
  A murmur into her music broke;
And she paused to hear, for she could but
      know
  The baby's angel spoke.

"Cheek or chin, or knuckle or knee,
Where shall the baby's dimple be?
Where shall my finger fall and rest
When I come down to the baby's nest?
Where shall my finger's touch remain
When I awaken your babe again?"

Silent the mother sat, and dwelt
  Long in the sweet delay of choice;
And then by her baby's side she knelt,
  And sang with pleasant voice:

"Not on the limb, O angel dear!
For the charm with its youth will disappear;
Not on the cheek shall the dimple be,
For the harboring smile will fade and flee;
But touch thou the chin with an impress
    deep,
And my baby the angel's seal shall keep."

THE HEART OF THE WAR.

(1864.)

PEACE in the clover-scented air,
  And stars within the dome;
And underneath, in dim repose,
  A plain, New England home.
Within, a murmur of low tones
  And sighs from hearts oppressed,
Merging in prayer, at last, that brings
  The balm of silent rest.

———

I've closed a hard day's work, Marty,—
  The evening chores are done;
And you are weary with the house,
  And with the little one.
But he is sleeping sweetly now,
  With all our pretty brood;
So come and sit upon my knee,
  And it will do me good.

Oh, Marty! I must tell you all
  The trouble in my heart,
And you must do the best you can
  To take and bear your part.
You've seen the shadow on my face;
  You've felt it day and night;
For it has filled our little home,
  And banished all its light.

I did not mean it should be so,
  And yet I might have known
That hearts which live as close as ours
  Can never keep their own.
But we are fallen on evil times,
  And, do whate'er I may,
My heart grows sad about the war,
  And sadder every day.

I think about it when I work,
  And when I try to rest,

And never more than when your head
  Is pillowed on my breast;
For then I see the camp-fires blaze,
  And sleeping men around,
Who turn their faces toward their homes,
  And dream upon the ground.

I think about the dear, brave boys,
  My mates in other years,
Who pine for home and those they love,
  Till I am choked with tears.
With shouts and cheers they marched away
  On glory's shining track,
But, Ah! how long, how long they stay!
  How few of them come back!

One sleeps beside the Tennessee,
  And one beside the James,
And one fought on a gallant ship
  And perished in its flames.

And some, struck down by fell disease,
  Are breathing out their life;
And others, maimed by cruel wounds,
  Have left the deadly strife.

Ah, Marty! Marty, only think
  Of all the boys have done
And suffered in this weary war!
  Brave heroes, every one!
Oh! often, often in the night,
  I hear their voices call:
"*Come on and help us. Is it right*
  That we should bear it all?"

And when I kneel and try to pray,
  My thoughts are never free,
But cling to those who toil and fight
  And die for you and me.
And when I pray for victory,
  It seems almost a sin
To fold my hands and ask for what
  I will not help to win.

Oh! do not cling to me and cry,
  For it will break my heart;
I'm sure you'd rather have me die
  Than not to bear my part.
You think that some should stay at home
  To care for those away;
But still I'm helpless to decide
  If I should go or stay.

For, Marty, all the soldiers love,
  And all are loved again;
And I am loved, and love, perhaps,
  No more than other men.
I cannot tell—I do not know—
  Which way my duty lies,
Or where the Lord would have me build
  My fire of sacrifice.

I feel—I know—I am not mean;
  And, though I seem to boast,
I'm sure that I would give my life
  To those who need it most.

Perhaps the Spirit will reveal
  That which is fair and right;
So, Marty, let us humbly kneel
  And pray to Heaven for light.

———

Peace in the clover-scented air,
  And stars within the dome;
And underneath, in dim repose,
  A plain, New England home.
Within, a widow in her weeds,
  From whom all joy is flown,
Who kneels among her sleeping babes,
  And weeps and prays alone!

TO A SLEEPING SINGER.

LOVE in her heart, and song upon her lip—
A daughter, friend, and wife—
She lived a beauteous life,
And love and song shall bless her in her
  sleep.
The flowers whose language she interpreted,
The delicate airs, calm eves, and starry skies
That touched so sweetly her chaste sym-
  pathies,
And all the grieving souls she comforted,
Will bathe in separate sorrows the dear
  mound,
Where heart and harp lie silent and pro-
  found.
Oh, Woman! all the songs thou left to us
We will preserve for thee, in grateful love;
Give thou return of our affection thus,
And keep for us the songs thou sing'st
  above!

SONG AND SILENCE.

"My Mabel, you once had a bird
In your throat; and it sang all the day!
But now it sings never a word:
    Has the bird flown away?

"Oh sing to me, Mabel, again!
Strike the chords! Let the old fountain
    flow
With its balm for my fever and pain,
    As it did years ago!"

Mabel sighed (while a tear filled and fell,)
"I have bade all my singing adieu;
But I've a true story to tell,
    And I'll tell it to you.

"There's a bird's nest up there in the
    oak,
On the bough that hangs over the stream,
And last night the mother-bird broke
    Into song in her dream.

"This morning she woke, and was still;
For she thought of the frail little things
That needed her motherly bill,
        Waiting under her wings.

"And busily, all the day long,
She hunted and carried their food,
And forgot both herself and her song
    In her care for her brood.

"I sang in my dream, and you heard;
I woke, and you wonder I'm still;
But a mother is always a bird
    With a fly in its bill!"

ALONE!

ALL alone in the world! all alone!
With a child on my knee, or a wife on
    my breast,
Or, sitting beside me, the beautiful guest
Whom my heart leaps to greet as its sweet-
    est and best,
    Still alone in the world! all alone!

With my visions of beauty, alone!
Too fair to be painted, too fleet to be
    scanned,
Too regal to stay at my feeble command,
They pass from the grasp of my impotent
    hand:
    Still alone in the world! all alone!

Alone with my conscience, alone!
Not an eye that can see when its finger
 of flame
Points my soul to its sin, or consumes it
 with shame!
Not an ear that can hear its low whisper
 of blame!
 Still alone in the world! all alone!

In my visions of self, all alone!
The weakness, the meanness, the guilt that
 I see,
The fool or the fiend I am tempted to be,
Can only be seen and repented by me:
 Still alone in the world! all alone!

Alone in my worship, alone!
No hand in the universe, joining with mine,
Can lift what it lays on the altar divine,
Or bear what it offers aloft to its shrine:
 Still alone in the world! all alone!

In the valley of death, all alone!
The sighs and the tears of my friends are
      in vain,
For mine is the passage, and mine is the
      pain,
And mine the sad sinking of bosom and
      brain :
  Still alone in the world! all alone!

Not alone! never, never alone!
There is one who is with me by day and
      by night,
Who sees and inspires all my visions of
      light,
And teaches my conscience its office aright:
  Not alone in the world! not alone!

Not alone! never, never alone!
He sees all my weakness with pitying eyes,
He helps me to lift my faint heart to the
      skies,
And in my last passion he suffers and dies :
  Not alone! never, never alone!

ALBERT DURER'S STUDIO.

IN the house of Albert Durer
　Still is seen the studio
Where the pretty Nurembergers
　(Cheeks of rose and necks of snow)
Sat to have their portraits painted,
　Thrice a hundred years ago.

Still is seen the little loop-hole
　Where Frau Durer's jealous care
Watched the artist at his labor,
　And the sitter in her chair,
To observe each word and motion
　That should pass between the pair.

Handsome, hapless Albert Durer
　Was as circumspect and true

As the most correct of husbands,
    When the dear delightful shrew
Has him, and his sweet companions,
    Every moment under view.

But I trow that Albert Durer
    Had within his heart a spot
Where he sat, and painted pictures
    That gave beauty to his lot,
And the sharp, intrusive vision
    Of Frau Durer entered not.

Ah! if brains and hearts had loop-holes,
    And Frau Durer could have seen
All the pictures that his fancy
    Hung upon their walls within,
How minute had been her watching,
    And how good he would have been!

THE OLD CLOCK OF PRAGUE.

THERE'S a curious clock in the city of
    Prague—
A remarkable old astronomical clock—
With a dial whose outline is that of an
    egg,
    And with figures and fingers a wonder-
    ful stock.

It announces the dawn and the death of
    the day,
    Shows the phases of moons and the
    changes of tides,
Counts the months and the years as they
    vanish away,
    And performs quite a number of mar-
    vels besides.

At the left of the dial a skeleton stands;
  And aloft hangs a musical bell in the
    tower,
Which he rings, by a rope that he holds
    in his hands,
  In his punctual function of striking the
    hour.

And the skeleton nods, as he tugs at the
    rope,
  At an odd little figure that eyes him
    aghast,
As a hint that the bell rings the knell of
    his hope,
  And the hour that is solemnly tolled is
    his last.

And the effigy turns its queer features away
  (Much as if for a snickering fit or a sneeze),
With a shrug and a shudder, that strug-
    gle to say:

" Pray excuse me, but—just an hour more,
  if you please ! "

But the funniest sight, of the numerous
    sights
  Which the clock has to show to the peo-
    ple below,
Is the Holy Apostles in tunics and tights,
  Who revolve in a ring, or proceed in a
    row.

Their appearance can hardly be counted
    sublime ;
  And their movements are formal, it must
    be allowed ;
But they're prompt, for they always appear
    upon time,
  And polite, for they bow very low to the
    crowd.

This machine (so reliable papers record)
Was the work, from his own very clever
 design
Of one Hanusch, who died in the year
 of our Lord
  One thousand four hundred and ninety
  and nine.

Did the people receive it with honor? you
 ask ;
 Did it bring a reward to the builder ?
 Ah, well !
It was proper that they should have paid
 for the task !
 And they did, in a way that it shocks
 me to tell.

For suspecting that Hanusch might grow
 to be vain,
 Or that cities around them might covet
 their prize,

They invented a story that he was insane,
And, to stop him from labor, extin-
guished his eyes!

But the cunning old artist, though dying
in shame,
May be sure that he labored and lived
not amiss;
For his clock has outlasted the foes of his
fame,
And the world owes him much for a
lesson like this:

That a private success is a public offence,
That a citizen's fame is a city's disgrace,
And that both should be shunned by a
person of sense,
Who would live with a whole pair of
eyes in his face.

A CHRISTMAS CAROL.

THERE'S a song in the air!
There's a star in the sky!
There's a mother's deep prayer
And a baby's low cry!
And the star rains its fire while the Beau-
tiful sing,
For the manger of Bethlehem cradles a
king.

There's a tumult of joy
O'er the wonderful birth,
For the virgin's sweet boy
Is the Lord of the earth,
Ay! the star rains its fire and the Beau-
tiful sing,
For the manger of Bethlehem cradles a
king!

In the light of that star
Lie the ages impearled ;
And that song from afar
Has swept over the world.
Every hearth is aflame, and the Beautiful
    sing
In the homes of the nations that Jesus
    is King.

We rejoice in the light,
And we echo the song
That comes down through the night
From the heavenly throng.
Ay! we shout to the lovely evangel they
    bring,
And we greet in his cradle our Saviour
    and King!

VERSES READ AT THE HADLEY CENTENNIAL.

(*JUNE* 9, 1859.)

HEART of Hadley, slowly beating
  Under midnight's azure breast,
Silence thy strong pulse repeating
  Wakes me—shakes me—from my rest.*

Hark! a beggar at the basement!
  Listen! friends are at the door!
There's a lover at the casement!
  There are feet upon the floor!

But they knock with muffled hammers,
  They step softly like the rain,
And repeat their gentle clamors
  Till I sleep and dream again.

* The pulsations of Hadley Falls, on the Connecticut, are felt for many miles around, in favorable conditions of the atmosphere.

Still the knocking at the basement;
  Still the rapping at the door;
Tireless lover at the casement;
  Ceaseless feet upon the floor.

Bolts are loosed by spectral fingers,
  Windows open through the gloom,
And the lilacs and syringas
  Breathe their perfume through the room.

'Mid the odorous pulsations
  Of the air around my bed,
Throng the ghostly generations
  Of the long forgotten dead.

" Rise and write ! " with gentle pleading
  They command and I obey;
And I give to you the reading
  Of their tender words to-day.

" Children of the old plantation,
   Heirs of all we won and held,
Greet us in your celebration—
   Us—the nameless ones of Eld!

" We were never squires or teachers,
   We were neither wise nor great,
But we listened to our preachers,
   Worshipped God and loved the State.

" Blood of ours is on the meadow,
   Dust of ours is in the soil,
But no marble casts a shadow
   Where we slumber from our toil.

" Unremembered, unrecorded,
   We are sleeping side by side,
And to names is now awarded
   That for which the nameless died.

"We were men of humble station;
  We were women pure and true;
And we served our generation,—
  Lived and worked and fought for you.

"We were maidens, we were lovers,
  We were husbands, we were wives;
But oblivion's mantle covers
  All the sweetness of our lives."

"Praise the men who ruled and led us;
  Carry garlands to their graves;
But remember that your meadows
  Were not planted by their slaves.

"Children of the old plantation,
  Heirs of all we won and held,
Greet us in your celebration,—
  Us, the nameless ones of Eld."

This their message, and I send it,
  Faithful to their sweet behest,
And my toast shall e'en attend it,
  To be read among the rest.

Fill to all the brave and blameless
  Who, forgotten, passed away!
Drink the memory of the nameless,—
  Only named in heaven to-day!

WANTED.

GOD give us men! A time like this de-
    mands
Strong minds, great hearts, true faith, and
    ready hands;
Men whom the lust of office does not kill;
  Men whom the spoils of office cannot buy;
Men who possess opinions and a will;
  Men who have honor,—men who will not
    lie;
Men who can stand before a demagogue,
  And damn his treacherous flatteries with-
    out winking!
Tall men, sun-crowned, who live above the
    fog
  In public duty, and in private thinking:
For while the rabble, with their thumb-
    worn creeds,

Their large professions and their little
    deeds,—
Mingle in selfish strife, lo! Freedom weeps,
Wrong rules the land, and waiting Justice
    sleeps!

MERLE THE COUNSELLOR.

OLD MERLE, the counsellor and guide,
And tall young Rolfe walked side by side
At the sweet hour of eventide.

The yellow light of parting day
Upon the peaceful landscape lay,
And touched the mountain far away.

The tinkling of the distant herds,
And the low twitter of the birds
Mingled with childhood's happy words.

The old man raised his trembling palm,
And bared his brow to meet the balm
That fell with twilight's dewy calm:

And one could see that to his thought,
The scenes and sounds around him brought
Suggestions of the heaven he sought.

But Rolfe, his young companion, bent
His moody brow in discontent,
And sadly murmured as he went.

For vagrant passions, fierce and grim,
And fearful memories haunted him,
That made the evening glory dim.

Then spoke the cheerful voice of Merle:
" Where yonder clouds their gold unfurl,
One almost sees the gates of pearl.

" Nay, one can hardly look amiss
For heaven, in such a scene as this,
Or fail to feel its present bliss.

" So near we stand to holy things,
And all our high imaginings,
That faith forgets to lift her wings!"

Then answered Rolfe, with bitter tone:
"If thou hast visions of the throne,
Enjoy them; they are all thy own.

".For me there lives no God of love;
For me there bends no heaven above;
And Peace, the gently brooding dove,

" Has flown afar, and in her stead
Fierce vultures wheel above my head,
And hope is sick and faith is dead.

" Death can but loose a loathsome bond,
And from the depths of my despond,
I see no ray of light beyond."

It was a sad, discordant strain,
That brought old Merle to earth again,
And filled his soul with solemn pain.

At length they reached a leafy wood,
And walked in silence, till they stood
Within the fragrant solitude.

Then spake old Merle with gentle art:
"I know the secret of thy heart,
And will, if thou desire, impart."

Rolfe answered with a hopeless sigh,
But from the tear that brimmed his eye,
The old man gladly caught reply,

And spoke: "Beyond these forest trees
A city stands; and sparkling seas
Waft up to it the evening breeze.

"Thou canst not see its gilded domes,
Its plume of smoke, its pleasant homes,
Or catch the gleam of surf that foams

"And dies upon its verdant shore,
But there it stands; and there the roar
Of life shall swell for evermore!

"The path we walk is fair and wide,
But still our vision is denied
The city and its nursing tide.

"The path we walk is wide and fair,
But curves and wanders here and there,
And builds the wall of our despair.

"Make straight the path, and then shall
        shine
Through trembling walls of tree and vine
The vision fair for which we pine.

"And thou, my son, so long hast been
Along the crooked ways of sin,
That they have closed, and shut thee in.

"Make straight the path before thy feet,
And walk within it firm and fleet,
And thou shalt see, in vision sweet

"And constant as the love supreme,
With closer gaze and brighter beam,
The peaceful heaven that fills my dream."

He paused: no more his lips could say;
And then, beneath the twilight gray,
The silent pair retraced their way.

But in the young man's eyes a light
Shone strong and resolute and bright,
For which Merle thanked his God that night.

DANIEL GRAY.

IF I shall ever win the home in heaven
For whose sweet rest I humbly hope and pray,
In the great company of the forgiven
I shall be sure to find old Daniel Gray.

I knew him well; in truth, few knew him
      better ;
For my young eyes oft read for him the
      Word,
And saw how meekly from the crystal letter
He drank the life of his beloved Lord.

Old Daniel Gray was not a man who lifted
On ready words his freight of gratitude,
Nor was he called upon among the gifted,
In the prayer-meetings of his neighborhood

He had a few old-fashioned words and
    phrases,
Linked in with sacred texts and Sunday
    rhymes;
And I suppose that in his prayers and graces,
I've heard them all at least a thousand times.

I see him now—his form, his face, his mo-
    tions,
His homespun habit, and his silver hair,—
And hear the language of his trite devotions,
Rising behind the straight-backed kitchen
    chair.

I can remember how the sentence sounded—
" Help us, O Lord, to pray and not to
    faint!"
And how the " conquering-and-to conquer "
    rounded
The loftier aspirations of the saint.

He had some notions that did not improve
    him,
He never kissed his children—so they
    say ;
And finest scenes and fairest flowers would
    move him
Less than a horse-shoe picked up in the
    way.

He had a hearty hatred of oppression,
And righteous words for sin of every kind ;
Alas, that the transgressor and transgres-
    sion
Were linked so closely in his honest mind !

Yet that sweet tale of gift without repent-
    ance,
Told of the Master, touched him to the core ;
And tearless he could never read the sent-
    ence :
"Neither do I condemn thee: sin no more."

He could see nought but vanity in beauty,
And naught but weakness in a fond caress,
And pitied men whose views of Christian
    duty
Allowed indulgence in such foolishness.

Yet there were love and tenderness within
    him ;
And I am told that when his Charley
    died,
Nor nature's need nor gentle words could
    win him
From his fond vigils at the sleeper's side.

And when they came to bury little Charlie,
They found fresh dew-drops sprinkled in his
    hair,
And on his breast a rose-bud gathered
    early,
And guessed, but did not know who placed
    it there.

Honest and faithful, constant in his calling,
Strictly attendant on the means of grace,
Instant in prayer, and fearful most of fall-
    ing,
Old Daniel Gray was always in his place.

A practical old man, and yet a dreamer,
He thought that in some strange, unlooked-
    for way
His mighty Friend in Heaven, the great
    Redeemer,
Would honor him with wealth some golden
    day.

This dream he carried in a hopeful spirit
Until in death his patient eye grew dim,
And his Redeemer called him to inherit
The heaven of wealth long garnered up for
    him.

So, if I ever win the home in heaven
For whose sweet rest I humbly hope and
    pray,
In the great company of the forgiven
I shall be sure to find old Daniel Gray.

THE MOUNTAIN CHRISTENING.

(A Legend of The Connecticut.)

How did they manage to busy themselves—
    Our sires, in the early plantation days?
Grinding their axes and whittling their
    helves?
    Fishing for salmon and planting maize?

–

How when the chopping and splitting were
    done?
    How when the corn-fields were planted and
    hoed?
How when the salmon had ceased to run,
    And the bushes were cleared from the old
    Bay Road?

They were not men who stood still in their
    shoes,
  Or who clung to their cabins when forests
      were damp ;
So, when labor was finished, they cut the
    blues
  And their sticks for a lively exploring
      tramp.

'Twas a beautiful morning in June, they
    say—
  Two hundred and twenty years ago,
When armed and equipped for a holiday,
  They stood where Connecticut's waters
      flow,

With five upon this side and five upon
    that,—
  Agawam's bravest and hardiest men,
Hailing each other with lusty chat,
  That the tall woods caught and tossed
      over again.

Holyoke, the gentle and daring, stood
  On the Eastern bank with his trusty four,
And Rowland Thomas, the gallant and good,
  Headed the band on the other shore.

"Due North!" shouted Holyoke and all
    his men.
  "Due North!" answered they on the
    opposite beach ;
And northward they started, the sturdy ten,
  With their haversacks filled and a musket
    each.

The women ran panting to bid them good-
    bye
  And sweet Mary Pynchon was there (I
    guess),
With a sigh in her throat and a tear in
    her eye
  As Holyoke marched into the wilderness,

And the boys were all wondering where
    they would go,
  And what they would meet in the dan-
    gerous way ;
And the good wives were gossiping to and
    fro,
  And prating and shaking their heads all
    day

Up the bright river they travelled abreast,
  Calling each other from bank to bank,
Till the hot sun slowly rolled into the West,
  And gilded the mountain-tops where it sank.

They lighted their camp-fires and ate of their
    fare,
  And drank of the water that ran at their
    feet,
And wrapped in the balm of the cool evening
    air,
  Sank down to a sleep that was dreamless
    and sweet.

The great falls roared in their ears all night,
  And the sturgeon splashed and the wild-
    cat screamed,
But they did not wake till the morning
    light
  Red through the willowy branches beamed.

Brief was the toilet and short the grace,
  And strong were the viands that broke
    their fast;
Then onward they pressed till they reached
    the place
  Where the river between two mountains
    passed.

Up the rough ledges they clambered amain,
  Holyoke and Thomas on either hand,
Till high in mid-passage they paused, and
    then
  They tearfully gazed on a lovely land.

Down by the Ox-Bow's southerly shore
  Licking the wave bowed an antlered buck ;
And Northward and Westward a league or
    more
  Stretched the broad meadows of Nono-
    tuck.

Straight up the river an Indian town
  Filled the soft air with its musical hum,
And children's voices were wafted down
  From the peaceful shadows of Hockanum.

                                        •

Rude little patches of greening maize
  Dappled the landscape far and wide,
And away in the North in the sunset's blaze,
  Sugar-loaf stood and was glorified !

The morning dawned on the double group
  Facing each other on opposite shores,
Where ages ago with a mighty swoop
  The waters parted the mountain doors.

"Let us christen the mountains," said Holy-
　　oke in glee ;
　"Let us christen the mountains," said
　　Thomas again ;
"That mountain for you, and this mountain
　　for me!"　　　　　　　　　　　·
　And their trusty fellows responded :
　　"Amen!"

Then Holyoke buried his palm in the
　　stream,
　And tossed the pure spray toward the
　　mountain's brow,
And said, while it shone in the sun's first
　　beam,
　"Fair mountain, thou art Mount Holyoke
　　now!"

The sun shone full on the Western height,
　When Thomas came up from the crystal
　　tide :

^a I name thee Thomas by Christian rite !"
  " Thou art Mount Thomas !" they all
    replied.

They paused but a moment when rounding
    a bluff
Shot an Indian's boat with its stealthy oar,
And with strings of wampum and gaudy stuff
  They beckoned it in to the Western shore.

Gracious and brief was the bargain made
  By the white man's potent pantomime ;
And the delicate boat with its dainty blade
  Bore them over the river one man at a
    time.

There were greetings and jests in every
    mouth,
  And hearty farewells to " Holyoke " and
    " Tom ":

Then the gleeful men turned their steps due
   South,
   And took a bee-line for Agawam.

They passed Willimansett at noon that day,
   And Chicopee just as the sun went down,
And when the last daylight had faded away,
   All hungry and weary they entered the
   town.

Mr. Pynchon demanded a full report,
   Which Holyoke wrote for the two com-
   mands;
And when he went down to the General
   Court
   He placed it in Governor Winthrop's
   hands.

A GOLDEN WEDDING-SONG.

The links of fifty golden years
  Reach to the golden ring
Which now, with glad and grateful tears,
  We celebrate and sing.
O chain of love! O ring of gold!
  That have the years defied;
And still in happy bondage hold
  The old man and his bride!

The locks are white that once were black;
  The sight is feebler grown;
But through the long and weary track
  The heart has held its own!
O chain of love! O ring of gold!
  That time could not divide;
That kept through changes manifold
  The old man with his bride!

The little ones have come and gone;
  The old have passed away;
But love—immortal love—lives on,
  And blossoms 'mid decay.
O chain of love! O ring of gold!
  That have the years defied;
And still with growing strength infold
  The old man and his bride!

The golden bridal! ah, how sweet
  The music of its bell,
To those whose hearts the vows repeat
  Their lives have kept so well!
O chain of love! O ring of gold!
  O marriage true and tried!
That bind with tenderness untold
  The old man to his bride!

OLD AND BLIND.

GALLANT Gray-beard, can't you see
   You unconscionable bat, you—
While you play the devotee,
   That the girl is laughing at you ?

You were handsome in your day,
   You are well preserved and thrifty,
And your manners, one may say,
   Are superb, but—you are fifty !

Don't be foolish, now you're old,
   Flirting in this feeble fashion,
Trying on a hearth grown cold
   To re-light a boyish passion.

You have had your day of youth,
    With its tender freaks and fancies ;
You have known a woman's truth,
    And have lived Love's sweet romances.

Ay, I know her lips are red ;
    True, her curls are black and glossy ;
Yes, she bears a dainty head,
    And her eyes are sweet and saucy.

But she knows you act a part,
    While you try to tease and please her,—
Knows, Old Make-believe, your heart
    Is as dead as Julius Cæsar ;—

Knows it, though a simple girl,
    And is laughing while you linger ;—
Knows it well, and, like a curl,
    Winds you round her jewelled finger !

But if you must act a part ;
   If you cannot drop your feigning,
Feign you have not in your heart
   Such a thing as love remaining.

Come and stand with me, my friend,—
   She'll permit you—never doubt her !
Do as I do, and pretend
   Not to care a fig about her !

HER ARGUMENT.

"DONALD'S dead," she murmured, smiling,
 as she met me at the door.
 "Come and see the little fellow ere we
 carry him away!"
Then she turned with queenly gesture, and
 walked firmly on before,
 To the chamber where the coffin and its
 lovely burden lay.

She was not of earth that morning; she was
 up among the spheres—
 Cloud and darkness underneath, and round
 her paradisal air—

For her eyes had seen a vision that forbade
    their falling tears,
And her heart had framed an argument
    that banished her despair.

Smiling lips and waxen forehead, folded
    hands and pulseless breast,
There he lay—the household treasure—to
    be hidden ere the night !
And the mother stood above him with her
    hands together pressed
In a rapture of thanksgiving—in a trans-
    port of delight !

Then she spoke : "An angel met him at the
    parting of his breath,
For he reached his hands up swiftly, and
    he answered with a smile !

Ah my Donald, darling Donald ! Thou art
    conqueror of death !
  Evil cannot now ·disturb thee, nor the
    touch of sin defile.

" Do not stray too far, my Donald ! Linger
    for me on the hills !
  Oh, there's time enough for straying !
    Wait and see it all with me !
I shall go to thee when graciously the
    Heavenly Father wills,
  And I know that I shall know thee, when-
    soever it may be ! "

I had come to bring her comfort, but I stood
    in dumb amaze,
  For her peace was like a river and her joy
    too full for speech.

I had come to lead her sobbing through the
    dim and doubtful ways
That philosophy discloses and the hack-
    neyed schoolmen teach.

She had learned a better logic ; she was mis-
    tress of the hour ;
And I stood before her, humbled, know-
    ing that my scheme was vain.
" Tell me, woman," said I, trembling—" tell
    me, if thou hast the power,
How thou knowest that this little boy of
    thine shall live again ? "

" Sweetest thing in earth and heaven "—
    made she answer to my quest—
  " Life of Godhead, breath of angels, every
    good and gift above,

Was bestowed upon my Donald—lived and
    throbbed within his breast—
God had given him love for largess, and
    had given him power to love !

" If He had not loved my Donald, would He,
    think you, have bestowed
What was best in all His kingdom—what
    was royal and divine—
On the little earthly nature, till I knew it the
    abode
Of the presence of The Master, and revered
    it as a shrine ?

" God is bountiful, but gives not gifts like
    this to stocks and stones !
His are all the living creatures on a thou-
    sand happy hills ;

But He only gives them pleasure, and a
place to hide their bones
When decay descends upon them, or the
cruel hand that kills.

" Would He fit a soul to love Him, and give
nothing in return ?
Would He care a soul should love Him if
He did not love it well ?
Love must find a love that answers, or with
hopeless passion learn ;
And God loves us, or our love is but the
mockery of hell.

" This is certain as the sunlight, this is true
as life is true :
And no soul can frame conception of a
being so inane,

That, with power to save, He wills not to
    recover and renew
  Every object of His tenderness that falls
    in mortal pain !

"Oh I know it : God loved Donald ; and
    He will not let him die.
  Even I had saved him living if my love
    had had the might.
Did the God of earth and heaven love my
    darling less than I ?
  Having loved him will He damn him to
    the everlasting night?

" That is not the way of loving. Every in-
    stinct of love's power
  Moves to shield its precious object from
    destruction and decay ;
And I know that God loved Donald, and
    that Donald has for dower
  Immortality of being, in the everlasting
    day ! "

A LEGEND OF LEAP YEAR.

"No poet should invent his own romance."—*Stedman.*

      " *One, two,*
        Buckle my shoe."
Two little shoes with silver buckles dight,
Lay in the room where she had passed the
      night.
She raised them in her fingers, pink and
      white,
And put them on her feet, and strapped
      them tight.

      " *Three, four,*
        Open the door."
Then slowly rising from her cushioned chair,
She gave a last deft crinkle to her hair,
And oped the door and hurried down the
      stair—
Her petticoats soft rustling through the air!

" *Five, six,*
  Pick up sticks."
Straight to the yard she skipped on queenly
    toes,
To where in serried ranks the wood-pile rose,
Then piled her arm with hickory to her nose,
And bore it to the house through air that
    froze.

" *Seven, eight,*
  Lay 'em straight."
At length the wood was blazing on the fire,
Though still unequal to her fierce desire ;
And so she punched and punched the cheer-
    ful pyre,
And heaped with sticks the household altar
    higher.

" *Nine, ten,*
  Good fat hen."
And then the eager hunger-fiend was foiled,
And she was glad, indeed, that she had
    toiled ;
For when her hands were washed, so sadly
    soiled,
She sat down to a last year's chicken—
    BROILED !

" Eleven, twelve,
  Toil and delve."
Then to her waist her pink of pinafores
She fastened, and did up her little chores,
Made soap, made bread, baked beans, and
    swept her floors,
And worried through a hundred household
    bores.

" Thirteen, fourteen,
  Girls are courtin'."
Next morn before her door the grocer's van
Drove up. 'Twas leap-year, and she laid
    her plan.
So when he asked for orders, she began
To blush, and said she'd take a market-man !

" Fifteen, sixteen,
  Girls are fixin'."
She overhauled her linen-chest with pride,
Bought hose, bought gloves, bought sheet-
    ings two yards wide,

Bought blankets and a hundred things be-
    side
That woman buys when she becomes a bride.

    " *Seventeen, eighteen,*
      Girls are waitin'."
And then she waited—waited day by day,
Till weeks had flown, and months had passed
    away,
But still her order lingered in delay,
Although she longed to have it filled—and
    pay.

    " *Nineteen, twenty,*
      Girls are plenty."
At length she knew. *Embarras de richesses*
Had thrown the fellow into wild distress,
And he had gone to drinking to excess,
Crushed by the weight of offered loveliness.

She called and saw him, selling by the pound
Within his stall. "Fact is," said he, " **I**
    found
That gals this year so wonderful abound,
No single market-man won't go around ! "

FALSE AND TRUE.

THE false is fairer than the true.   Behold
Yon cloudy giant on the hills supine !—
The figure of a falsehood that doth shine,
Armored and helmeted, in such a gold
As in the marts was never bought or sold,—
Giant and armor the exalted sign
Of shapes less glorious and tints less fine—
Of forms of truth outmatched a thousand
      fold !
Ah, Poesie !   Thou charmer and thou cheat !
Painting for eyes that fill with happy tears,
In tints delusive, pictures that repeat
Dull, earthly forms in heavenly atmospheres !
How dost thou shame the truth, till it ap-
      pears
Less lovely far than thy divine deceit !

THRENODY.

OH, sweet are the scents and songs of spring,
  And brave are the summer flowers ;
And chill are the autumn winds, that bring
  The winter's lingering hours.
And the world goes round and round,
  And the sun sinks into the sea ;
And whether I'm on or under the ground,
  The world cares little for me.

The hawk sails over the sunny hill ;
  The brook trolls on in the shade ;
But the friends I have lost lie cold and still
  Where their stricken forms were laid.

And the world goes round and round,
  And the sun slides into the sea ;
And whether I'm on or under the ground,
  The world cares little for me.

O life, why art thou so bright and boon !
  O breath, why art thou so sweet !
O friends, how can ye forget so soon
  The loved ones who lie at your feet !
But the world goes round and round,
  And the sun drops into the sea,
And whether I'm on or under the ground,
  The world cares little for me.

The ways of men are busy and bright ;
  The eye of woman is kind :
It is sweet for the eyes to behold the light,
  But the dying and dead are blind.

And the world goes round and round,
  And the sun falls into the sea,
And whether I'm on or under the ground,
  The world cares little for me.

But if life awake, and will never cease
  On the future's distant shore,
And the rose of love and the lily of peace
  Shall bloom there for evermore,
Let the world go round and round,
  And the sun sink into the sea !
For whether I'm on or under the ground,
  Oh, what will it matter to me ?

TO MY DOG "BLANCO."

My dear, dumb friend, low lying there,
A willing vassal at my feet,
Glad partner of my home and fare,
My shadow in the street,

I look into your great brown eyes,
Where love and loyal homage shine,
And wonder where the difference lies
Between your soul and mine !

For all of good that I have found
Within myself or human kind,
Hath royally informed and crowned
Your gentle heart and mind.

I scan the whole broad earth around
For that one heart which, leal and true,
Bears friendship without end or bound,
And find the prize in you.

I trust you as I trust the stars;
Nor cruel loss, nor scoff of pride,
Nor beggary, nor dungeon-bars,
Can move you from my side !

As patient under injury
As any Christian saint of old,
As gentle as a lamb with me,
But with your brothers bold ;

More playful than a frolic boy,
More watchful than a sentinel,
By day and night your constant joy
To guard and please me well,

I clasp your head upon my breast—
The while you whine and lick my hand—
And thus our friendship is confessed,
And thus we understand !

Ah, Blanco ! did I worship God
As truly as you worship me,
Or follow where my Master trod
With your humility,

Did I sit fondly at His feet,
As you, dear Blanco, sit at mine,
And watch Him with a love as sweet,
My life would grow divine !

TWO HOMES.

I HASTEN homeward, through the gathering
    night,
Tow'rd the dear ones who in expectance
    sweet
Await the coming of my weary feet,
With faces in the hearth-fire glowing bright,
And please my heart with many a lovely
    sight
Of way-worn neighbors, stepping from the
    street
Through doors thrown wide, and bursts of
    light that greet
Their entrance, painting all their paths with
    white ;
And then I think, with a great thrill of bliss,
That all the world, and all of life it brings,
Tell me true tales of other realms than this,
As faithful types of spiritual things ;
And so I know that home's rewarding kiss
Insures the hope of heaven that in me springs.